HOMICIDE IN BLACK AND WHITE

The first in

The Tanner and Thibodaux Action Adventure Series

Larry Watts

Lone Writer Publishing

Homicide in Black and White
A Tanner & Thibodaux Action Adventure

Copyright © March 2014 by Larry Watts

First edition May 2014

Inquiries to
Lone Writer Publishing
2874 Morning Pond Lane
Dickinson, TX 77539

ISBN – 978-0-9890859-3

Library of Congress Control Number: 2014906764

This is a work of fiction. All characters depicted herein are fictional and the product of the author's imagination. All events portrayed are also fictional.

Published in the United States

As with all my writing, special thanks to my wife, Carolyn, a fellow author and inspirational partner.

Thanks also to my author friends Rene' Palmer Armstrong, Gloria Hander Lyons, and Tom Rizzo for their editing, titling and cover design advice.

Chapter 1

At twenty, Hunter Hansen was a lucky young man. For three decades, the Hansen family made its home in Success, Texas. His parents, Hobart and Vanessa, were high achievers, a perfect match for a town with such a name.

Hunter's great-grandfather, Hollister Hansen, had made a fortune in the oil business, back in the early days of SpindleTop and other giant Texas oil fields. He had diversified his holdings into banking, with small independent banks in several rural communities. After moving his family to Success, he opened the bank that the next two generations of Hansen men had been identified with.

The jury was still out on whether Hunter would be the fourth generation of bankers. After high school he enrolled at the University of Texas, but was a student there for less than two months before being suspended. The campus police charged him with aggravated assault after an altercation with a female student who refused to allow him in her dorm room following their first date.

His father saw to it that the criminal charges were dropped. He could not, however, prevent the expulsion, because the victim also came from an affluent Texas family.

After being kicked out of college, Hunter returned to Success, where he spent his time much as he had while in high school. His father put him on the bank payroll, ostensibly to train as a bank teller. Hunter, however, had no interest in working at the bank. He arrived to work late, if at all. After a few weeks he was ignored by the head teller, who knew she had to approve his paychecks, but didn't intend to waste her time scheduling work he wouldn't do. Both were happy with her logic.

*****

Danielle Parker knew she was in trouble. She never should have gotten involved with Hunter Hansen. Hunter was more than three years her senior and there was still a racial divide in rural Texas. Oh, sure, there were interracial marriages and plenty of light-skinned kids living in and around Success; she was one herself. But when they married, the white spouse was considered white trash and the black soon learned the hard lesson that just marrying a white doesn't get you moved across the tracks. She knew that was why Hunter usually insisted that he pick her up in the alley at the end of her street. He often drove from there to a secluded hunting cabin his dad owned just outside of town.

Danielle was sixteen years old. She knew she was pretty. But when the son of Success's most prominent citizen started flirting with her, she had been shocked. It started one evening after school when she stopped by the Community Center, a hang-out for teens and young adults. Most parents considered it to be a safe a place for their sons and daughters to congregate.

Hunter, who was bored shooting pool with high school boys, noticed her when she walked in. He couldn't believe he'd never really looked at her before. She was elegant. Her body had the fully-rounded curves of a woman. Without intending to, she demanded attention when she came into the room. And just when he thought a woman couldn't be that beautiful, he saw her eyes. They were emerald green and a perfect match for her bronze skin, the color that white girls spent hours in the sun trying to attain. Hunter knew she was black, but he was mesmerized.

She was flattered when the older boy, and white at that, began flirting with her that night. She stayed later than usual at the Center, simply because she loved the attention. When she left, Hunter followed her out and offered to drive her home. She started to refuse, because she knew if her mother saw a white boy dropping her off, she would be angry. But Danielle couldn't resist. Hunter had dropped her on the street beside her house, after making a date to meet the next afternoon.

The dating had continued, though never in public. At first it was just driving around town or out into the country. Hunter soon suggested that they go to his father's hunting cabin where he drank beer and introduced Danielle to smoking marijuana. On

3

the third trip to the cabin, Hunter convinced her to have sex with him.

Their relationship had been difficult, in part because he was very demanding of her time and her body. He insisted that she perform sexual acts that she had never even heard of before. It scared her, but she was drawn to the son of one of the most respected families in the county. If he wanted her, she was sure that she could rise above the poverty and get to the other side of the tracks, the unspoken dream of those who resided in Success's project housing neighborhoods, if they managed to avoid addiction to meth or other street drugs.

But there was another reason that the relationship suffered. Neither was prepared to inform their families, much less make it public. Hunter was an adult, but he lived in an apartment building owned by his father, and Hobart Hansen controlled the lives of his entire family. Hunter knew that if his father learned he was dating a black, his paycheck from the bank would be cut off and he would be on his own. Danielle feared that she would suffer the worst fate she could imagine; her mother's rejection.

Tonight she had to tell him. She had considered talking to her uncle, Calvin Thibodaux, first, but decided not to. She got herself in this mess; she'd have to handle it. The doctor had confirmed it. She was pregnant.

They met in the parking lot of the Community Center. Danielle got in Hunter's truck and he headed for the cabin. She didn't say a word. Finally he looked at her.

"What's the matter with you?"

"Nothing that can't wait until we get there," she replied.

They rode in silence for the fifteen minutes it took to drive to the cabin. Once there, Hunter unlocked the cabin door and they entered. He took a beer from the refrigerator, sat on the couch and began removing his boots. Danielle stood at the door and watched him.

"Come on, get undressed, girl," Hunter motioned toward the bed.

"We've got to talk, Hunter. I'm pregnant."

With one boot off, he froze with his still booted foot resting across his knee. After a moment, he spoke.

"So, whose is it? Can't be mine. I wear a rubber every time." He proceeded to remove the second boot.

She was surprised and hurt that his reaction was so cold. She had known he'd be angry, but to suggest that she had been with someone else was something she hadn't expected.

"You know it's yours! Why would you say that? I love you." She walked from the door to stand in front of him.

"Get your clothes off. I guess I don't need a rubber now." He stood and pushed her toward the bed.

"NO! We need to talk about this! We're not going to bed!"

She was surprised at the anger in her voice, but the look on Hunter's face turned the anger into fear as he removed the boot.

"Let me tell you something, nigger girl. You'll damn well do as I tell you and do it now!"

He rose from the couch and swung his arm in a wide arc as he backhanded her across the cheek. She fell onto the bed and he was on top of her instantly, tearing at her clothes. When her blouse tore and revealed her breasts, he became more excited. He raised his body to a kneeling position on the bed, unzipped and pushed down his jeans as he leaned over her.

"Do it! You know what I want."

He thrust toward her face, grabbing her hair and pushing himself inside her mouth. She was crying and tried to roll away, but he was too strong. A hard shove and she was on her back. He ripped at her panties after lifting her skirt. She struggled and he began to hit her face. She screamed. He wrapped his fingers around her neck and began to squeeze, harder and harder.

As he peered down at her face, he realized he had gone too far. The beautiful green eyes were bulging and she was no longer screaming. He

6

squeezed harder and wrenched her head to the side. When he let go, she didn't move.

"Stupid nigger bitch! Why'd you make me do that?" Hunter spoke as if he believed she could hear him.

He zipped his pants and put his boots on. After sitting on the edge of the bed for a few seconds, he walked to the refrigerator and opened another beer. He returned to the couch where he sat, drank the beer, and stared at Danielle's dead body.

When the beer was gone, Hunter took a deep breath, rose from the couch and took three steps to the bed and rolled the girl's body to the edge. He then lifted her over his shoulder and carried her to his truck, where he dumped the body into its bed as if she were a sack of flour.

Hunter jumped into the truck and drove back to the main road. He turned left, away from town, and drove a half mile to the Colorado River. Veering slightly right, off the highway, he drove down a dirt lane, parking beneath the bridge. He got out of his truck, lowered the tailgate and pulled Danielle's stiffening body from the bed. Hunter carried her to the edge of the river and dropped the body on the river's bank. With a shove of his boot, the body slid into the shallow water.

Chapter 2

The Sheriff, Justice of the Peace, and three deputies were under the bridge where Danielle's body had been dumped. It was a little after five the morning after Hunter dumped Danielle's body at the river's edge.

One of the deputies was talking with the fisherman who had discovered the girl's body and called 911. As they pulled the corpse from the shallow water of the river, it shifted to the side and the Sheriff found himself staring into the face of Danielle Parker.

"Well, boys, it's going to be a bad day for Estelle Parker. That's Danielle and she's Estelle's pride and joy."

Sheriff Randy Jackson had been on many similar scenes. He'd been a San Antonio homicide detective before retiring and returning to his home town to run for sheriff.

"Boss, I don't see any sign of a struggle here. Lots of tire tracks, but everybody that's got a fish hook has been down here at one time or another. You want us to tape it off and try to get Ted Braniff out here?"

The young deputy was referring to the Texas Ranger assigned to this and several adjoining counties.

"I'd rather get the DPS forensic people out. But, I'll make that call myself. Tape it off and stay here. I'm heading back to town. I'll visit with Estelle first and then call DPS."

The Sheriff walked to his car and drove away in a cloud of dust. Twenty minutes later, when he pulled into the driveway of Estelle Parker's home, he noted how well-kept it was compared to the other homes in the neighborhood. Estelle Parker, like her half-brother Calvin Thibodaux, was a cut above the norm for the residents of the 'bottoms.' That's the tag put on the area of town west of the railroad tracks. It used to be all black, but now it was a mix of poor blacks, meth-addicted whites, and a smattering of Mexicans and Vietnamese. He got out of his car and began the dreaded walk to her front door.

When Estelle answered the door, Sheriff Jackson removed his white cowboy hat. She knew something was wrong before he spoke.

"Estelle, can I come in?"

She opened the screen, stood to the side and asked, "What's happened Sheriff? It's Danielle, isn't it? Where is she?"

"Danielle was found by a fisherman out under the river bridge on FM 109 early this morning, Estelle. I'm sorry."

Estelle screamed, "No! Not my girl!"

The Sheriff caught her arm as she began to collapse and led her to the couch, where she sank into the cushion sobbing.

"Estelle, you've got to stay strong for a few minutes now. I've got to ask you some questions. When did you see her last?"

"When she got home from school yesterday. She came in and said she was going to the Community Center. She goes there a lot. She didn't come home before dark, so I started calling her friends, but they hadn't seen her."

"Did you call the police or our office?" The Sheriff asked.

"I called the Success police, but they told me she was probably just out with friends, said they wouldn't report her missing until she was gone 24 hours."

Estelle lost her composure again and began to cry, emitting guttural sounds of anguish.

The Sheriff sat and patted her hand for a moment, before asking, "Did she have a boyfriend?"

"Danielle was friends with all the boys and all the girls. She was concentrating on her school work. She's never asked me if she could date. Why would anybody want to hurt her?"

"We're going to find out, Estelle. Can I call Calvin over here to be with you?" The Sheriff stood to leave.

"He's supposed to come over this morning to mow the yard. Where they taking my baby, Sheriff? I got to be with her."

Sheriff Jackson explained that there would be an autopsy; when the body was released she would

11

need to choose a funeral home to pick up Danielle's body. Then he left, hoping Calvin got there soon.

It was a long day for the Sheriff and the two deputies he assigned to assist with the homicide investigation. They set up an office at the high school and began interviewing Danielle's classmates. It wasn't long before they heard Hunter Hansen's name. Four students told similar stories. Danielle and Hunter often met at the Community Center parking lot and drove away together. No one knew where they went.

Success had never had a murder committed in town and the last one in Fulshear County had been five years earlier. That case had been easy; a husband shot his wife's ex-husband during an argument about child support. The husband was charged and pled guilty in a plea arrangement that got him five years.

Sheriff Jackson knew this one was going to be more difficult. He met with the deputies when the school interviews were complete and decided that he would question Hunter Hansen himself. The deputies were instructed to go to Hunter's apartment first thing the following morning and bring him to the Sheriff's office.

At eight o'clock the next morning, Jackson stood outside the interrogation room peering in at Hunter through the one-way glass. Hunter looked more irritated than worried. The Sheriff opened the door and entered the room, sitting across the table from him.

"Hunter, I guess you know why I asked my deputies to bring you here. You've heard about Danielle Parker?"

"I heard about it, but why do you want to talk to me? I don't know anything about her."

The Sheriff smiled at the younger man as he said, "I hear that you've spent quite a lot of time with her recently. Isn't that true, son?"

Before Hunter could answer, there was a knock on the door and a deputy opened it.

"Sheriff, can you step out here?"

Jackson rose and stepped from the room, shutting the door as he walked out.

"Carter Prevost is here. Says Hunter is his client and is demanding to see him before any questioning takes place. He's in your office." The deputy waited for instructions.

"No problem, deputy. I'll handle it."

The Sheriff walked to his office, entered and saw the attorney seated against the wall.

"Hello, Carter. You're out awfully early this morning. What can I do for you?"

The lawyer stood, extended his hand and as the two shook, began, "Hunter Hansen is my client. He's not speaking to you or your deputies, and unless you are charging him, I will take him home now."

"Well, I'm not charging him, because right now he's just another witness. So you're telling me that your client won't cooperate in finding Danielle Parker's murderer?"

"I'm telling you I want to see my client. If you have questions, we will respond to them at my office. Call my secretary to set a time, if you wish. Now, can I see my client?"

"Sure Carter. Follow me." The Sheriff walked out, followed by the lawyer. When they stepped into the interrogation room the Sheriff spoke first.

"Hunter, I guess we'll postpone our talk. Seems your lawyer wants to be present and he's invited us to his office to have that conversation. You're free to go."

The lawyer and his client left the Sheriff's office. Jackson told his secretary to set an appointment with Prevost's office to interview Hunter. The Sheriff believed that "lawyering up" so early in an investigation usually cast more suspicion on a person, but not always.

Chapter 3

Late on the morning that Danielle's body was discovered, Milo Tanner heard the doorbell ring as he was going out the back door. He ignored the sound, stepped out the door, and walked around to the front. There was his friend, Calvin Thibodaux, a thin, light-skinned black man, standing on his front porch.

Dressed in blue jeans and a Houston Texans t-shirt, his friend always looked fastidious. His jeans were clean and had been starched and ironed with a well-defined crease down the middle of each leg. Tanner remembered the first time he met Calvin Thibodaux thinking that he had not seen blue jeans so crisp, creased and starched in the last fifteen years. The stress was apparent on his friend's face.

"Tanner, my Danielle's been murdered. I'm going to need your help before this is over."

*****

As Tanner stood there looking at his friend, his mind drifted back again to the very first time he had met Calvin Thibodaux. Much like this morning, he had knocked on Tanner's front door.

"Good mornin', suh," Thibodaux had said, "My name is Calvin Thibodaux. I saw you just moved in here and wanted to introduce myself. I did the yard work for Ms. Taylor who owned the house fo' you moved in. I'd be glad to do your yard work, too."

"How much did you charge Ms. Taylor and what did you do?" Tanner had asked.

"I mowed, edged the sidewalk and trimmed the bushes when they needed it for thirty-five dollars each week. During the winter, we'd just do it ever' two or three weeks. That's what I'd charge you, too."

"Let's give it a try. Can you do it today?"

"Yes, suh, I just need to go home and get my mower." Thibodaux had turned and walked away.

Thirty minutes later, Tanner heard the lawn mower beside his office window. He pulled back the curtain and saw that Thibodaux had parked a riding lawn mower with a small trailer attached, on the street in front of his house. The trailer had several lawn tools in it. The yard was small and Thibodaux was maneuvering a smaller lawn mower back and forth across it.

Thibodaux had knocked again at the front door in less than an hour. Tanner invited him in, but noticed the other man's hesitancy before entering.

"Sit down while I get your money. You want a bottle of water or a beer?" Tanner asked as he walked to his desk.

"Yes, suh, a bottle of water would be nice." Thibodaux remained standing.

Tanner picked up the money clip from beside his computer and walked to the refrigerator where he took out a bottle of cold water. He came back to Thibodaux, who stood in the entry way, just outside the room Tanner used as an office. He had peeled off thirty-five dollars and handed it with the water to his new yard man.

"What do people call you?" he had asked.

"Most folks just call me Calvin, but some call me Thibodaux, 'cause of my last name."

"Well, I like the name Thibodaux, so that's your name with me. You been around here long?" Tanner had asked.

"Pretty much grew up here, went to the Army for twenty years and then right back here. I still live in the house my mama raised me in. She's passed now, but I'm still here," Thibodaux responded.

"Well, I just moved here from Houston. I wanted to retire in a small town and this place filled the bill for that. Just drop by every Friday for the lawn work. Thanks."

Tanner held out his hand and Thibodaux took it. He walked out the door, mounted his riding lawn mower and was off to his next job. A friendship was born that morning.

Milo Tanner had bought the home after turning in his retirement papers to the Houston Police Department. He wrapped up his personal business in the big city and moved to his new home in Success, Texas, population of 3,952. For twenty-five years he had worked as a police officer, nineteen as a detective investigating robberies and homicide cases. He was drawn to Success because of its size and its name.

Many small Texas towns have great names. He looked in Dime Box, Cut 'n Shoot, Palestine, Big Foot, and several others, but he liked Success best. About ninety miles west of Houston, the median income was just above the poverty level, but there was a pleasant feel about the town. After finding the home for sale, he bought it without hesitation-- reasonably sure this place would provide the serenity he hoped to enjoy now that he didn't have to cope with Houston's daily rationing of homicides, robberies and drug deals.

The house was on a narrow street with trees lining both sides creating a canopy of shade all the way across. Three blocks north was the downtown square, consisting of two banks, several antique stores, a liquor store, a couple of real estate offices and a small hamburger joint. At least half the store front businesses were vacant and had "For Sale or Lease" signs in the windows.

About an equal distance to the east of Tanner's new home ran the Colorado River, just at the edge of town. The banks of the winding river were overgrown with willow trees and other plants that thrived in such close proximity to the plentiful supply of water at the river's edge. There were a few homes built above its steep banks, but a significant portion of the river bank had been undisturbed for years, with the occasional exception of a few young boys braving the high weeds and mosquitoes to camp out for a night.

The Friday morning after first meeting Thibodaux, a half-hour before noon, Tanner heard the buzz of the lawn mower again. He had just returned from what he thought to be the best restaurant in town, Tex's World Famous BBQ. He'd bought enough barbequed ribs, link sausage, potato salad and red beans to feed half his neighborhood. Tanner had a weakness for good barbeque and always bought enough for several meals. He decided to invite the yard man to eat with him when the work was finished.

When Thibodaux knocked on the front door, Tanner invited him in. The two men sat at the kitchen bar and ate barbecue. As their conversation grew more personal, Tanner told Thibodaux about his work at the police department and Thibodaux related his family history in Success. Tanner noticed that as the conversation continued, Thibodaux's southern black dialect began to disappear.

"So, Thibodaux, you grew up here in Success, but I don't understand the Cajun last name. It's a name you're more likely to hear in Houston and farther east into Louisiana."

Tanner was genuinely interested. His curiosity had served him well as an investigator. He had learned early on that people like to talk about themselves. Asking the right questions was a habit he would not soon break. His questions for

Thibodaux, however, were simply to satisfy his personal desire to get to know the people in his new hometown.

"My daddy was Carl Thibodaux. He came through Success when my mama was just 14 years old. He stayed for two years doing farm work. He left one day and we never heard from him again. I don't even remember him. I wasn't a year old when he left," Thibodaux told Tanner. "I ain't got but two relatives left alive. That's my half-sister, Estelle Parker, and her daughter, Danielle, prettiest girl in Success!"

Thibodaux reached for his wallet and flipped it open to show Tanner a photo of his niece, a beautiful, light-skinned teenager, with sparkling emerald green eyes.

"Pretty girl," Tanner remembered saying.

"She's a real good kid. What about you, Mr. Tanner? You got any family?"

"First, don't call me Mr. I'm just Tanner. My wife and I had no children. She left me ten years ago. It's just me now." Tanner stared into space for a moment, before continuing to eat his barbecue.

*****

As the months passed, Tanner and Thibodaux became fast friends. Thibodaux sometimes brought his niece with him to help with the yard care. Danielle was pretty and smart. It was obvious that she wanted to please her uncle and the feeling was mutual.

Tanner learned that when Thibodaux retired from the military, he had returned to Success and begun mowing lawns. Soon it became a full-fledged landscaping business, but he did all the work himself, except for Danielle's part-time assistance. Thibodaux still liked to travel, a practice he attributed to his military career. He was planning a trip to Europe and told Tanner that when he had the money together, he would be gone for a month. Danielle would take care of his customers while he was away.

Tanner's first impression had been that Thibodaux was just a local boy whose life was much like other black residents in Success. But as he learned more about him, he realized that was not the case at all. One day Tanner finally asked a question that had bothered him for some time.

"Thibodaux, that day I first met you, there was a strong black southern dialect to your speech. It wasn't long before you lost that altogether. What's that about?"

Thibodaux smiled, "Oh, Mista' Tanner, you means why'd I talk like this? Well, let me tells you."

Tanner interrupted him, "That's even worse than that first day. I prefer the real Thibodaux."

"Well, Tanner," Thibodaux became serious as he spoke. "Around here, it's sometimes easier to be who people expect you to be. Some of my customers, all white, would be uncomfortable dealing with an educated black man. They're not bad people. That's just the environment they've been in most of their lives, with blacks on one side of the tracks and whites on the other.

"I knew after I got to know you that it would be okay to be myself. Few people in Success know that I have a bachelor degree from Penn State. I got it while I was a Ranger in the Army.

"No need to tell them now. I'll go on letting them think I'm just old Calvin Thibodaux who grew up here and never changed during all those years I was gone. I know who I am, and that's what matters."

When Thibodaux finished speaking, he leaned against the pecan tree where they were standing.

"You're an interesting man, Thibodaux. I'm glad I met you," Tanner replied.

"You probably need to know that some people here may not like you inviting me in your house and socializing with me. It's just not the way things are done here in Success." Thibodaux picked a pecan off the ground as he spoke.

"I don't have part-time friends, Thibodaux. I choose who I associate with."

Thibodaux gathered his tools and the two men walked to the front yard, where Thibodaux mounted his lawn mower and took off for another job.

Chapter 4

Tanner's thoughts of the past were interrupted as Thibodaux repeated, "I know you can help." Tanner opened the door for him.

"Tell me what you know," he said, motioning for his friend to take a seat. "Did the Sheriff tell you anything about it yet? Who did it?"

"Not much from the Sheriff. Fisherman found her out under the bridge on the old farm to market road. I heard this morning that Danielle had been running around with the Hansen kid. Haven't told Estelle yet. The problem will be even worse when she learns that."

Tanner's brow furrowed, "Why will that make it worse, Thibodaux? I know you still see a racial divide here in Success, but each generation is going to blur the black and white distinction more and more."

"Oh, our family has been doing that for a while. Danielle's father was Hobart Hansen. Estelle never told her. Apparently Danielle had the same attraction to the Hansen's that her mother did." Thibodaux stared at the floor for a moment.

"Estelle was in love with Hobart when she got pregnant while he was home from college. He'd married Vanessa Brown right out of high school and they had Hunter soon after. They went off to college, but he came back by himself about three years later when his grandmother got sick.

"Hobart told Estelle some line about having divorced Vanessa. She was just nineteen, gullible, and thought that racial divide didn't exist any longer. She believed him and got herself in a mess, getting pregnant. His daddy sent him back to college as well as to his wife and child after Hobart told him Estelle was pregnant. When he came back, he never spoke to her again, far as I know. She never got married; just spent all her time taking care of Danielle and working at the school cafeteria."

"That would complicate things. I'm really sorry for you and Estelle. If there's anything I can do, let me know. I think I'll drop by the Sheriff's office tomorrow and see what I can learn."

"I'd appreciate your doing that, Tanner. But I have to tell you, if a Hansen's involved, not much will be done officially. That may be why I need your help," Thibodaux said.

Tanner wasn't ready to buy into his friend's theory that a wealthy family would be untouchable when it came to murder.

"Let's see how things develop, Thibodaux. There's been a murder and it won't be ignored, that's for sure."

Thibodaux thanked Tanner and left the house to return to his sister's home.

*****

The next morning Tanner drove to the Fulshear County Law Enforcement Center and parked in a visitor's space. He smiled when he realized he had never entered a "cop shop" as a visitor before. He hadn't met the Sheriff since moving to Success, but figured it was a good time.

Tanner entered the lobby and approached the reception clerk. She sat behind a thick glass with a speaker system and sliding drawer in the lower portion.

"Hi, my name's Milo Tanner. I moved to Success several months ago from Houston, when I retired from the P.D. there. Any chance I could visit with Sheriff Jackson for a few minutes?"

"Let me see if he's in," the receptionist said as she picked up the phone.

The Sheriff had just concluded his conversation with Prevost and Hunter Hansen before walking back to his office. When the receptionist told him a retired Houston cop was waiting to see him, he welcomed what he thought would be a diversion from the murder case.

"Milo Tanner," he said, extending his hand to the Sheriff who rose from his chair behind a desk.

The two men shook as the Sheriff said, "I'm Randy Jackson. I understand you're retired from HPD. Welcome to Fulshear County. I retired from San Antonio before getting elected sheriff, so we share a common background. Have a seat."

The Sheriff motioned toward one of two chairs in front of his desk as he sat.

"Sheriff, I..." Tanner began as he too lowered himself into one of the chairs, but was interrupted.

"Call me Randy," the Sheriff insisted.

"Randy, I moved here several months ago and made a few acquaintances. One of them is a gentleman by the name of Calvin Thibodaux. The girl you found yesterday is his niece." Tanner paused.

"I know Calvin," the Sheriff responded. "Matter of fact he was a year ahead of me in high school. I grew up here in Success, you know."

"No, I didn't know that. What I really came by for was to see if I might learn a little about the investigation." Tanner saw the momentary change in the Sheriff's facial expression.

"You know, it's really early and we're still working the scene where the body was found. DPS forensics team is out there now. Not much to tell you, really."

Tanner sensed that the Sheriff didn't want to be rude to his new constituent, maybe because he was a fellow retired cop, but he wasn't forthcoming with much information.

"What about suspects? I hear she was dating the son of Hobart Hansen. I'd think it's pretty unusual in a small town, black girl from over the tracks, dating the son of the wealthiest man in the county, or so I hear anyway."

26

Tanner watched closely as he spoke, but the Sheriff had no visible reaction.

"I don't know about their dating, but I intend to talk to Hunter. My secretary is setting it up as we speak. Look, you know I can't discuss the case with you. It's a more sensitive matter in a small community than in Houston or San Antonio. It's a pleasure meeting you and when I get untangled from this murder case, maybe we can sit and visit."

Tanner rose from the chair.

"Thanks, Sheriff. I don't want to put you in a bad position; just thought you might have something. If I can help in any way, please let me know."

He removed a card from his shirt pocket and handed it to the Sheriff. The Sheriff looked at the card. Written on it was simply 'Tanner' with a phone number below the name.

"I'll let you know if there's anything you can do," the Sheriff said as he rose and walked around the desk.

The men shook hands and Tanner returned to the parking lot. He was on his way home minutes after the meeting.

Chapter 5

As the initial investigation was drawing to a close on the third day after Danielle's body was discovered, the Sheriff and two deputies reviewed their findings. There was little physical evidence at the scene, except for the body. The initial conclusion of the medical examination was that the victim had been strangled. Although the torn clothing indicated a possible sexual assault, there was no indication of sexual activity before or after the murder. The time of death was estimated to have been eight to twelve hours before the fisherman discovered the body. Five strands of hair, not believed to belong to the victim, were recovered from the body.

Two witnesses at the Community Center gave statements that they saw Danielle get into Hunter's truck at about four o'clock on the afternoon of the murder. One of the witnesses was a parent who had been dropping her son at the Center; the other was a classmate of Danielle's.

The Sheriff had an appointment to meet with Hunter Hansen at his attorney's office when the meeting with his deputies concluded. He had received calls from two county commissioners and the chairman of the Republican Party with inquiries concerning Hunter Hansen having been brought in for questioning. None of the three asked direct questions about the investigation, nor did they accuse Sheriff Jackson of any impropriety; but it was clear that Hobart Hansen was sending a message.

As he drove to Carter Prevost's office, he considered the differences in his previous investigations as a local cop and this one. Even though he had investigated several high profile murder cases in San Antonio, politicians had never exerted political pressure directly on him.

He wasn't concerned about the calls. His contract with the voters lasted four years. He couldn't be fired. He had run as a Republican simply because in Texas, you had to run on one ticket or the other; and Democrats had a dismal record of getting elected for the last twenty years. He would call the shots on the investigation and to hell with Fulshear County politics.

When he arrived at Prevost's office, the lawyer and his client were waiting. He was ushered into a conference room large enough to accommodate a dozen people around a long table. Hunter and Carter Prevost were already seated.

"Sheriff, you know my client, Hunter Hansen. He's here today to assist you in any manner we can to determine who killed Danielle Parker. Please ask him whatever you like."

"Hello, Hunter. Let's start with the question you didn't get to answer last time. Were you and Danielle Parker seeing each other?"

Hunter looked at Prevost before answering, "Yes."

"Did you see her on the evening before her body was found?"

As if reading from a script, Hunter said, "Yes. I picked her up at the Community Center about four o'clock. We drove around for an hour or so and I dropped her off in the alley behind her house."

Jackson tried not to let the surprise show on his face. Carter Prevost had taken his client to the woodshed before their meeting. Hunter was well prepared to answer the questions.

The Sheriff continued, "How long had you been seeing Danielle?"

"About three months."

"What kind of relationship was it?"

Carter Prevost placed his hand on Hunter's and said, "Sheriff, we don't understand that question. What do you want to know?"

"Were the two of you having sex?" the Sheriff asked.

"We had sex." Hunter's responses remained mechanical.

"How many times?"

Hunter smiled at the Sheriff, "Every time I could get her pants down and that was easy enough to do."

The Sheriff had interviewed dozens of over-confident murder suspects; he recognized an opportunity and tried to take advantage of the answer.

31

"Oh, is that right, Hunter? When was the last time you had sex with her? Was it the night she was murdered?"

Hunter Hansen had gotten "off-script" with his last answer and his lawyer knew it.

Carter Prevost spoke, "Sheriff, Hunter did not have sex with the girl the last time he saw her. He picked her up at the community center, they drove around town for a while, during which time she told him she was pregnant. Hunter knew he didn't get her pregnant since he always took precautions. Once he told her that, she apparently decided her little ruse wouldn't work, so she asked him to take her home. That's what my client knows about this. Is there anything else?"

Jackson ignored the lawyer, "You know anybody else who was dating or having sex with Danielle, Hunter?"

"Sure she was having sex with other guys. How do you think she got pregnant? I don't know who, but then it's your job to figure that out isn't it, *Mister* Jackson?"

The Sheriff sat silently for a moment, looking alternately at the two men who sat across from him. Prevost was doing his job. He found no fault with that. Hunter Hansen, on the other hand, was a narcissistic punk. He may not have killed Danielle, but he could have.

"Make sure your client's available if I need to talk to him again, Carter." The Sheriff stood and walked from the room.

When Sheriff Jackson arrived back at his office, he received more news about the forensic evidence. Danielle Parker was pregnant at the time of her death, approximately 12 weeks along. DNA samples were taken from the fetus. Asphyxiation from choking was confirmed as the cause of death which did not take place in the water where she was found. He decided it was time to visit with the District Attorney.

*****

Jack Sadosky was not new at dealing with political issues in Fulshear County. He had been the District Attorney for 18 years. During that time, he had faced a wide array of decisions involving prominent citizens and political figures. At times he had become extremely innovative in finding reasons not to prosecute certain cases; those who pulled the strings in Fulshear County had shown their appreciation by returning him to office at each election.

He was so good at walking that line that he also had a reputation as being beyond reproach in his duties as district attorney. That reputation came largely as a result of his ability to re-direct the blame when he chose not to pursue a case. Someone else, past sheriffs, a state agency, or, in some cases, even the victim, was cast in the role of preventing Jack Sadosky from pursuing justice. As a result he had preserved his law and order reputation.

When Sheriff Jackson sat in the chair across from his desk, Sadosky knew they would be talking about the murder of Danielle Parker. It was the only matter being discussed throughout the county. Though rumors had already surfaced regarding Hunter Hansen's possible involvement, unsolved murders made people uncomfortable until someone was in jail.

"So have we solved the murder yet, Sheriff?"

"That's what I'm here to discuss, Jack. We're still waiting on some lab results. I'm sure you heard that Danielle was pregnant. We don't have DNA results on the fetus yet and I'm waiting for test results on the hairs recovered from the body."

The Sheriff went on to explain his circumstantial case on Hunter Hansen, including the two witnesses who saw him pick her up at the community center the night of the murder. He explained Hunter's admission to having a sexual relationship with Danielle and his assertion that he had dropped her off at her house at five that afternoon."

The Sheriff paused for a moment, before continuing, "I've received a few calls. Seems some folks are concerned about Hunter being a possible suspect. You been getting the same type of calls?"

Sadosky didn't hesitate, "I always get calls when a politician or a prominent family is involved in one of our criminal cases. We'll just proceed without letting that influence us. That sound about right to you, Sheriff?"

"That's why I came by. Just wanted to be sure we are on the same page, Jack. Political interference, no matter how subtle, isn't something I've much experience dealing with, but I'll tell you, it won't affect this investigation."

"It's the way I've always run the D.A.'s office. We'll wait for the remainder of the testing, maybe you'll develop more information while we wait, and then we'll take it to the grand jury. Our job is just to present the facts, and that's what we'll do." Sadosky stood, indicating the meeting was over.

As the Sheriff drove back to his office, he realized what a smooth operator the D.A. was. During his short time in office, he'd never had such an important case. But a few of his deputies, who had worked for Fulshear County much longer, told him that Sadosky always found a way to satisfy the power structure, even if that meant not prosecuting some good cases. This was going to be interesting.

Before he got to his office, Trevor Talbot called him. Trevor was his Chief Deputy, and was also retired from the San Antonio Police Department.

"Randy, where are you? We just got the lab results back."

"I'm pulling into the parking lot now. See you in two minutes." The Sheriff parked and jogged up the steps.

As he walked into his office, Trevor followed him with a hand full of paper.

"I just read this. It looks like the hair from the body was identified as that of a white male. We've also got the DNA results on the fetus, but, of course, we'll need the father's DNA to match it."

"So we need to get samples from Hunter Hansen. If he won't agree, we'll try to get a warrant. I'll call Prevost now to see what he says." Jackson reached for the phone on his desk and made the call.

Neither the Sheriff nor his Chief Deputy was surprised when Carter Prevost told them that his client would not provide hair samples for testing. He also wanted to know if Hunter was now a suspect.

Jackson smiled as he used the relatively new, politically correct response, "No, Carter; let's just call him a *person of interest*."

Chapter 6

It had been ten days since Danielle's body was discovered. Sheriff Jackson sat across the desk from the District Attorney.

"Jack, you're going to have to get the judge to issue a warrant to collect samples for hair analysis and DNA comparison from Hunter Hansen. Prevost won't agree to a voluntary submission."

"Not a problem, Sheriff. I'm just not sure we've got a case even if his hair and DNA match. It doesn't prove anything that he hasn't already told us. He had sex with her; he was with her hours before her death, which he'll say explains the hairs. It's a tough case." Jack Sadosky leaned back in his chair.

"So, Jack, are you saying you won't file on him, even if we get both matches?"

"Oh, no, Sheriff; we'll take it to a grand jury and let them decide. But it's a tough case."

"How about the meeting tonight, Jack; you going to be there?"

The Sheriff directed the conversation to a meeting that had been called by the local NAACP president to provide information to the community about the murder. Walter Johnson was the municipal court judge as well as the president of the NAACP. As judge, he handled traffic tickets written by the Success police department, working only two days each week. His standing in the community was much more influenced by his role with the NAACP.

"No, Sheriff, I won't be there. I'm not going to let Johnson politicize my decision on any legal matter, especially this one."

"That's an interesting perspective on Walter. I really don't view this meeting as an attempt to politicize the murder. I think the community wants to know what we're doing. I'm going to be there. I'll check with you tomorrow to see if you get the search warrant."

The Sheriff stood and walked out of the office.

*****

The meeting was held at the Community Center. As the Sheriff expected, the majority of those attending were black, but there was a sprinkling of white residents there. He noticed that Milo Tanner was in attendance, sitting with Calvin Thibodaux and Estelle Parker.

Walter Johnson walked to the podium and began speaking, "Ladies and gentlemen, this is a sad time for our community. Our children are not supposed to go before us. Estelle, each of us wants you to know we feel your loss."

There were a few *amens* from the audience as Johnson continued, "I asked the Sheriff, the District Attorney and the members of our Commissioners' Court to be here with us tonight and to tell us what they can about the investigation. Unfortunately, only

Sheriff Randy Jackson and County Commissioner Alton Blackwell could make it. Each of the others contacted me and advised that they had previous commitments. Sheriff, Commissioner, thank you for responding to this community's request. Now, Sheriff, I'd like to turn the podium over to you and ask that you tell us what you can."

The Sheriff rose from his seat on the front row, took the podium, and looked out at the audience for a moment before speaking.

"Estelle, I am so sorry for your loss. Calvin, I know you cherished your niece. We will do all we can to bring the person who did this to justice.

"As far as the investigation is concerned, we are still gathering and testing evidence. We have not identified a suspect yet, but when we do, we will pursue that person without mercy. I will try to answer questions now, but please, remember that this is an open investigation. I will be limited in what I can tell you."

A young black man stood in the rear of the room. "Why has Hunter Hansen still not been arrested? You may not be able to say it; but everyone in this room knows he killed Danielle. We expect justice!"

The young man remained standing as the Sheriff spoke, "With all due respect, sir, unless there is an eyewitness in this room who has not come forward, no one 'knows' that Hunter Hansen murdered Danielle. We have questioned him, as we have a dozen other persons. If the evidence tells us he, or anyone else, is the murderer, we will get them."

"Sheriff, you ain't been back in Success long, but you know as well as me, that if a white girl was murdered, and witnesses saw her leaving this building with a black boy just a few hours earlier, that black boy would be so far back in your jail that he couldn't see daylight! We want justice." The young man remained standing.

Walter Johnson stepped to the podium beside the Sheriff, "Terrell, we all hear what you're saying. But we don't just want the murderer in jail now. We want to make sure he stays there; let's let the Sheriff do his job."

The meeting wore on, with a few questions from parents who wanted more police presence at the Community Center and a few who asked how they could protect their children. There was tension in the room, but the meeting ended without incident.

As Tanner was walking out with his friends, the Sheriff touched his arm, "Can you and Calvin spare a minute?" he asked as he stepped to the side.

The two men followed him away from the doorway, where they had more privacy.

"I decided to give you guys a little status update, Milo, isn't it?" the Sheriff asked.

"My name's Milo, but everyone just calls me Tanner, if you don't mind." Tanner hadn't used his first name since grade school.

"No problem, Tanner. I thought it might be easier for Estelle to hear it at home from you, Calvin. It's not much, but I should have a search warrant tomorrow to get hair and other DNA samples from Hunter Hansen. No matter what some of the folks in here may think, I will go after the murderer, no matter who it is."

"We appreciate that, Sheriff. Lot of folks out here tonight really do believe that the Hansen family is untouchable. I sure hope they're not right. Do you know about Hunter Hansen's history of violence against women?" Tanner asked.

The Sheriff's face registered surprise, "What are you talking about?"

Well, it's nothing you'll find doing a criminal records check, but he was kicked out of college after assaulting a female student who refused to let him in her dorm room. Twice he's beaten young women who live in the 'bottoms.'

"One was a prostitute who wouldn't agree to some of his sexual perversions. That was about four years ago. She didn't go to the police, but after her brother started talking about it around town, she suddenly had enough money to move to Houston and start a new life. Problem was she moved, but didn't start the new life. Her name was Gloria Washington. I checked with Houston. She overdosed on heroin six months ago.

"The other was a fourteen year old, name of Twila Spencer. Her family lived the next street over from Estelle and Danielle. Story I got was Hunter started fooling around with her. She made him mad one day when she didn't want to get in his truck. He slapped her around, took her out by the dump, raped her and left her to get back on her own. The Spencer family moved to Austin shortly after that. Nice home close to Barton Springs and Mr. Spencer retired.

"Those are just stories that get passed along. I don't know what they'd say if you could talk to the families."

The Sheriff said he knew both families, "Thanks for the information. I'll check it out." As he walked away, the Sheriff was surprised by how much information Tanner had been able to attain since moving to Success.

The next morning Jack Sadosky called the Sheriff and advised that he had obtained the warrant. He had also contacted Carter Prevost, who agreed to have Hunter at the law enforcement center to provide hair and saliva samples that afternoon.

The Sheriff was surprised, "I was sure that if the judge gave us a warrant, Prevost would try to stop it with an appeal to a higher court."

"No, Sheriff. He knew they'd have to give samples. He just wasn't going to do it without a court order. His defense is still the same. When I talked with him earlier, he said as much. Didn't make any difference if his client's hair was on the body, because he already said he was intimate with

Danielle. His client doesn't believe she was pregnant with his child, but even if she was, he didn't kill her."

Two days later, the lab results were forwarded to the Sheriff. The hairs recovered from the body belonged to Hunter Hansen and he was also responsible for the pregnancy.

Jackson called the D.A. and after relaying the test results, added, "I've developed some interesting information on Hunter Hansen." He went on to tell Sadosky of his conversation with Tanner.

"Interesting," Sadosky responded, "but is it anything more than rumor?"

"I'm not sure yet. The Spencer family wouldn't talk to my deputy. I can't locate Gloria Washington's brother, but he wasn't a witness to what happened to her anyway. At any rate, I want to file murder charges against Hunter and bring him in."

"Sheriff, don't rush this thing. Let's allow the grand jury to hear the evidence and tell us when to move forward. If we get an indictment, you'll have plenty of time to make the arrest." Sadosky wasn't going to bite.

*****

The D.A. scheduled the grand jury to hear evidence on the Danielle Parker murder case two weeks later. The Sheriff and Sadosky had all their

43

files together the evening before the hearing, when the D.A. received a call from Carter Prevost.

"Jack, I understand the grand jury is looking at the Parker murder case tomorrow. Is that right?"

"That's right, Carter. Your boy want to testify to the grand jury?" Sadosky knew he wouldn't.

"Oh, no, we just want to make sure they hear everything. I have the names of four young men who say they had sex with Danielle Jackson. Two of them say they "tag-teamed" her about a week before she was killed. That's their term, not mine. The other two boys also say they were with my client out at his dad's hunting cabin playing poker from about 5:30 until midnight the night she was killed. Just wanted to make sure you had that information for the grand jury."

Jack Sadosky wasn't surprised. "Give me the names, Carter. I'll postpone making the presentation to the grand jury until the Sheriff can talk to your witnesses."

"Glad to, Jack; it's a good group of boys, all local. Jeremy Crocker and Bradley Hankins are the boys who did the little *ménage a trois* with the victim. Tad Bradford and Porter Jackson, no relation to the Sheriff, were with my client that evening. I hope this helps." Prevost ended the call.

When the D.A. relayed the information to the Sheriff, the response didn't surprise him.

"Jack, this is B.S. and you know it," the Sheriff began before being interrupted by the D.A.

44

"Sheriff, it's your job to investigate, not mine. I'm not going to ignore the information Carter Prevost provided, no matter how convenient it is to his client. Now if you think these boys will be perjuring themselves before a grand jury, we're going to need to know that."

The D.A. postponed the grand jury hearing so that the Sheriff could take statements from the new witnesses. A week later, he and his deputies had interviewed and taken statements from each of the young men. Crocker and Hankins were as arrogant as Hunter Hansen. Both from well-respected local families, they related their stories of the sexual exploitation proudly.

Jackson was just as self-confident in relating his story of the late-night poker game and drinking binge on the night of the murder. While Bradford told the same story, he was nervous and, in the Sheriff's opinion, a poor liar.

The grand jury was scheduled the following week, but both the D.A. and Sheriff were sure there would be no indictment. One reason was the new witnesses discovered by Prevost; the other was the grand jurors themselves.

Grand juries are appointed by local judges. This one had two local attorneys, the wife of the Republican Party chairman, a real estate broker, and the Director of the Chamber of Commerce among other prominent citizens. All were connected in some way to the Hansen family.

Once all the evidence, including the witness statements, was presented, the grand jury spent little time no-billing, or in layman's terms, not charging Hunter Hansen. However, the action didn't preclude the possibility to re-open the case and file charges later.

Chapter 7

It didn't take long until nearly everyone in Fulshear County knew that Hunter Hansen was not going to jail for killing Danielle Parker. Most of those who heard didn't have an immediate reaction, but a few did. Terrell Jones, the young man at the community meeting who demanded that Hunter Hansen be arrested, began rallying support for a demonstration. Some accused him of being an opportunist at the expense of Estelle Parker, but she made no comment and quietly continued to grieve.

Calvin Thibodaux's response was out of character for the man who most in Success thought they knew. He had always recognized the local social structure and conducted himself so as not to upset the balance. Thibodaux had presented himself as the community expected. But the death of his niece marked a change. Two days after the grand jury, he knocked on Tanner's door.

"Come in, Thibodaux. How's Estelle doing?"

"Estelle knows better than most that a Hansen isn't likely to be held accountable in this community. She's grieving over Danielle, but she's not surprised.

"I want to do something, Tanner. I can't let this happen twice to my family."

Tanner had come to know Thibodaux pretty well and he wasn't surprised that there would be a point at which he would want to take a stand.

"What do you have in mind?"

"I want to know what you think we can do to get Hunter charged with Danielle's murder. And then I'll want to know how we get him convicted. I won't let this thing lay. If that doesn't work, I'll take care of it myself."

Tanner's expression was one of deep thought, "Thibodaux, I'm not sure we can get him indicted, but we might. I doubt there's much chance at all of the D.A. convicting him of murder.

"There are no witnesses and he has answers for the forensic evidence. But if you want to give it a try, I'm with you. You need to know before we get into this, we're not the cops. My approach may be a little unconventional and it may not be pretty."

Thibodaux didn't hesitate, "Tanner, I can handle unconventional. I was in Afghanistan when we first went in after 9/11. It was my last tour before I cashed out. Not much I haven't seen or done. Over there we did what needed to be done and we had support all the way up; at least as high up as wanted to know about it. But this deal won't have the blessing of the government and I understand that."

Tanner began by laying out a plan to get the indictment.

"First, we would have to get those witnesses that Prevost found at the last minute to recant their statements. You can't do that by just going to talk to them."

The two men spent the next hour planning their first move. Tanner knew nothing at all about the four young men who had become alibi witnesses for Hunter Hansen. Thibodaux knew who they were and a little about their families, but nothing that would help them figure out which of the four would be the most likely to come clean.

They decided to start with Jeremy Crocker. He was a couple of years older than Hunter and his family owned real estate investments in Austin and San Antonio. Like Hunter, Jeremy was on the payroll of his father's company, but he actually had a real estate broker's license and apparently did some work, mostly connected to the San Antonio properties.

For several weeks, Tanner tailed Jeremy from the time he left home until he retired for the night. Thibodaux assisted with the job, allowing them to use two cars, lessening the likelihood of being spotted. They soon realized that Jeremy Crocker was oblivious to any possibility that someone might be watching him.

They learned his routine quickly. He never left Success on Mondays or Tuesdays. On Wednesdays, he always drove to San Antonio, where he visited several small strip shopping centers. He visited with each of the business owners for a short time, collecting rent from some, and usually inspecting the outside structures before leaving.

He always ended his day at a small strip center not far from the freeway he took back to Success. This center had several unrented spaces, but the attraction for Jeremy was a small night club on one end. He spent a couple of hours in the club, before beginning the return trip to Success, long after the sun had set.

One night, as he left the night club, Jeremy noticed that the glass door of the vacant space two doors down was open. He didn't recall it being open when he arrived. He stepped into the space and could see that a light was on in an office at the rear of the rental space. He walked down the hallway to turn the light off.

Just before he reached the door, the light went out and someone grabbed him from behind. In seconds, his head was covered with a burlap hood and he was shoved into the room where the light had been. Jeremy sensed that a second person was in the room as his arms were pulled behind his back and bound with plastic zip-lock ties. He was then shoved into a chair. When he tried to stand, he was hit beside the head with what felt like a large book. It startled him, but didn't hurt that much. The sound alone was enough to stop his attempt to stand.

He heard a man's muffled voice, "Jeremy, you want to get out of here tonight; you need to answer my questions. The first thing I want to know why you lied about having sex with Danielle Parker."

"Fuck you, man. You can't do this. Let me go." He tried to stand, but this time received a well-placed kick between his legs. He moaned and fell to the floor, writhing in pain.

After 30 seconds, the voice uttered a single word, "Why?"

Jeremy lay on the floor and didn't respond. Moments later he was lifted by his elbows and placed on the chair again. He heard what he thought was the sound of a knife being sharpened on a whetstone.

"What are you doing?" He screamed.

"Jeremy, you are going to tell us what we want to know. It's not personal. We are going to do whatever we must, for you to understand that there is no alternative." The voice was as calm as that of a funeral director.

He felt hands unbuckling his belt. His slacks were unbuttoned, the zipper pulled down, and then he was made to stand, as his pants fell to the floor. The sound of the knife and whetstone continued. Jeremy began sobbing.

"Don't do this. Please! I just did a favor for Hunter. I never had sex with that kid."

"Tomorrow you will go to the District Attorney and retract your statement. You won't talk about what happened tonight and if you do, I'll finish this."

He felt a tug at his wrist and his hands were free.

"Now, sit. Count to one hundred very slowly; then remove the hood and go home. Do not forget your instructions."

Five minutes later, Jeremy ripped the hood from his head, flung it in the corner, pulled his pants up and ran from the building to his car. As he exited the parking lot, Thibodaux walked into the vacant office space and retrieved the burlap hood.

Chapter 8

The next week, Tanner began tailing Tad Bradford as he moved about town. It was much simpler than it had been to figure out the routine of Jeremy Crocker.

The Bradford family owned a lumberyard and hardware store outside Columbus, Texas, which was about thirty-five miles from Success. Tad lived with his parents on their ranch halfway between the two towns. Each morning he left the ranch, drove to the hardware store, and spent the day assisting customers or running one of the cash registers.

Tad came into Success twice after work during the five days Tanner tailed him. On one occasion he met Porter Jackson and Hunter Hansen at *The Dry Gulch Saloon,* Success's only bar. The three played pool for three hours before Tad returned home. The other foray into town was apparently a shopping trip. He went to the Brookshire Brothers Grocery and returned home with two sacks of groceries.

On Friday, Tanner stopped by the Sheriff's office. The receptionist, recognizing him from his previous visit, buzzed him in.

Tanner tapped lightly on the open door of Randy Jackson's office.

The Sheriff rose from his chair,

"Come in. Come in. Have a seat, Tanner. We haven't seen much of you lately."

"For a retired cop, I stay pretty busy," Tanner responded, "Just thought I would drop by and see if there's been anything new on Danielle's murder case."

"Not really. Hunter Hansen's still the suspect, but I don't think we'll ever put enough together to charge him. At this point, we'd need an eye witness, and I doubt there was one.

"One of *his* witnesses, Jeremy Crocker came by. He told me he had received a couple of threatening phone calls and wanted to withdraw his statement. Naturally, I didn't do that, but if it ever goes to another grand jury, I don't know what he would say."

Tanner feigned a look of surprise as he asked the question he could answer himself, "Do you think that's enough to have another grand jury look at it, Sheriff?"

"Why? There's still three other witnesses. I talked to the D.A. after Crocker came in and he says that once they gave statements, the case against Hunter was probably permanently tainted, even if they all recanted. The defense would call each one of them. They would have to admit that they made those original statements. No matter what their explanations in front of a jury for retracting them, it creates a lot of doubt about whether Hunter Hansen was with them when the murder occurred."

"That's pretty much what I figured, Sheriff. Well, sometimes justice is outside our grasp. I guess this is one of those times." Tanner rose to leave, but continued talking, "By the way Sheriff, after those boys said they were with Hunter at the Hansen hunting cabin, did anyone go out there and take a look around?"

"I'm a step ahead of you there. I told Prevost we wanted to look at the cabin. He objected at first, but after talking with his client, they agreed to let us go in the cabin. Of course, Prevost made sure we knew that Hunter had brought Danielle out there several times before she was killed. We didn't find anything but a few hairs on the bed. Preliminary tests showed they were from a black female, but like I said, they already explained that with their admission that Danielle and Hunter had sex on that bed."

"I guess Prevost is the lawyer to call when you're in deep shit in Fulshear County," Tanner replied.

"You know, Tanner, some of the people who were at the meeting that night, believe there is some kind of conspiracy to keep Hunter Hansen out of jail. It's not a conspiracy; it's the system.

"If the apartment manager hadn't called Hobart Hansen right away when my deputies picked Hunter up, I might have had time to get his statement before Prevost got here. Based on what little Hunter said to me, he would have denied dating Danielle. He as much as said he barely knew her just before his lawyer interrupted us. Then that DNA and matching hair would have been great evidence.

But by the time I finally got to talk to him again, Carter Prevost had already constructed his defense. He did a damn good job, too. So a poor man, black or white, probably wouldn't have been so lucky; not because of a conspiracy by the D.A. and me, but because the system is set up to favor those who have the money and the education to beat it."

"Yeah, like I said, sometimes justice is just out of reach. Thanks for the visit, Sheriff."

Tanner left the Sheriff's office and drove to Thibodaux's house. Thibodaux was maneuvering his lawnmower and trailer into the garage as Tanner parked in the drive. The two men sat under a shade tree and talked.

"How's Estelle doing, Thibodaux?"

"Not so good." Thibodaux replied, "She just can't get past the murder, keeps trying to think what she could have done to prevent it. I set an appointment with a psychological counselor in Houston. I hope it helps. She just seems to have given up on life."

"How about you? Are you alright?" Tanner could see that Thibodaux wasn't doing so well either.

"Oh, I'm okay. As long as we're trying to make this thing right, I keep going. Danielle didn't deserve that. It's got to be made right though."

Tanner nodded, "I visited with the Sheriff earlier. Jeremy Crocker had been there. Said he was getting threatening phone calls and wanted to retract his statement.

"Problem is, the D.A. believes that once those statements were made, they tainted the case against Hunter permanently. Sheriff said probably the only way to get a murder charge and conviction would be if there was an eye witness or, of course, a confession."

"What can we do, Tanner? I have to make this right for Danielle. Surely you know some way to make a murder charge stick on him." Thibodaux's despair was evident in his voice.

"Look, Thibodaux. Sit on it for a few days. We'll figure something out." Tanner didn't have a clue, but he couldn't tell his friend.

Tanner didn't see Thibodaux again until the next Friday. He'd stopped trailing Tad Bradford since a retraction of his statement would have no effect the D.A.'s decision on the case against Hunter.

On Wednesday evening, he decided to go to the *Dry Gulch Saloon* for a beer. When he arrived, the five o'clock crowd was beginning to thin out. He went to the bar and ordered a Shiner Bock beer. As he looked in the mirror behind the bar, he saw that Jeremy Crocker and Tad Bradford were shooting pool at one of the two tables.

Tanner ordered a second beer at about the time a group of six men came through the door and headed to the pool tables. Porter Jackson, Bradley Hankins and Hunter Hansen were in the group. It wasn't long before all eight men were shooting pool and joking loudly among themselves. There were only five other customers in the place. Tanner and two other men sat at the bar. A man and woman had found a secluded table in a corner, where they sat nursing beers while engaged in a quiet conversation.

One of the men, whom Tanner didn't know, sank the eight ball ending the first game.

"Hey, Hunter, you been back to the 'bottoms' since the murder?" he asked, displaying a wide grin.

"Never go over there," Hunter said. "Those girls come to see me. They all want some of what I was giving Danielle."

Everyone laughed except Tad and Jeremy. Both tried to hide their discomfort with the conversation.

"I bet that Sheriff would like another shot at you. I hear he was a hotdog detective in San Antonio. Comes back home to Success and finds out we stick together." Porter Jackson continued the conversation.

Bradley Hankins looked across the pool table at Hunter.

"Now that it's all over, why don't you tell us about that night, Hunter? Was she a fighter?"

"Look, guys. My lawyer told me not to talk about it. All I'm going to say is, I'll see that Sheriff looking for a job next election. And that nigger, Terrell Smith, who had so much to say at the meeting they had, demanding that they throw me in jail, he's got one coming too. Now let's shoot pool and drink some beer."

Tanner was surprised by the lack of respect that was shown for the dead girl. This bunch really believed they were untouchable...and maybe they were in Fulshear County. They hadn't even noticed that he was in the bar and probably didn't care.

On Friday, when Thibodaux finished Tanner's yard work, he knocked on the door. Tanner invited him in and went to the refrigerator for two beers. They sat at the breakfast table.

"You think of anything we can do to make that murder case?" Thibodaux got right to the point.

"I'm out of ideas, Thibodaux." As he spoke, Tanner was thinking about the conversation he heard at the bar. "Sometimes sending one guy to prison doesn't solve the problem anyway. I think the best thing for all of us is to continue remembering Danielle as the beautiful girl she was, and honor her by getting on with our lives."

Thibodaux looked puzzled, "I don't get it. There has to be some justice, Tanner."

Tanner felt for his friend, but there was nothing to be done. He didn't know how to help Thibodaux and Estelle anymore.

Chapter 9

In the months that followed Jeremy Crocker's encounter with the mysterious men in San Antonio, he became less concerned about further repercussions. He couldn't figure out who might have threatened him, but he decided not talk to any of the others who had made statements to the Sheriff for Hunter. Surely if they had all been threatened, one of them would have said something.

Apparently the Sheriff had not told anyone about Jeremy trying to withdraw his statement. If Hunter or his father knew, they would be furious at him.

The five men had become even closer since the murder. They met at the *Dry Gulch Saloon* at least once a week. In what Jeremy thought was ironic, they also began meeting at the Hansen cabin monthly for a regular poker game. While they each maintained other friendships, the poker game was exclusive. No one else was ever invited. They rarely spoke of Danielle Parker, and when one of them did, it was usually late in the evening after heavy drinking. More often than not, a sick joke was directed at Tad Bradford because he was the only one who was uncomfortable with the subject.

One night just after they all arrived at the cabin, and before the game began, Hunter pounded the table with his beer bottle.

"Before I take everyone's money in the poker game, I want to discuss something. Do you all remember Terrell Smith?"

None of them had forgotten him. Everyone who lived in Fulshear County had heard of him. After Danielle's murder, he had become a spokesman for part of the black community. The group was mostly young, teenagers and young adults. They held in common a belief that the NAACP and its leader, Walter Johnson, had become too passive in speaking out about injustices, real and perceived, in the black community.

"My Dad got a call today from Walter Johnson. Johnson told him that Terrell's group is going to start holding a rally once a month at different locations around town. They're calling it the "Justice for Danielle" rally. First one is next week in front of our bank."

Hunter paused for effect. "Now Dad told me we need to just ignore them and they'll get tired after a while. But I'm not going to do that. It's time Terrell learned to keep his mouth shut."

Tad was the first to speak, "I don't want to hear anything about this." He stood to leave.

"Sit down, Tad. There's nothing to worry about. I'm just going to send a little message and I'm not asking you to do anything at all."

Tad slowly lowered himself into the chair as Hunter continued. "Any of the rest of you want to go along? He should be headed home about now."

"Does this mean no poker game tonight?" Porter Jackson asked.

Hunter looked around the table. "Not tonight, boys. I was kidding about taking your money."

Porter stood. "I'm in then. Is everybody in? How about you, Hankins?"

Bradley Hankins stood also. "Let's go."

Jeremy Crocker reluctantly stood with the others, but Tad didn't move.

"I'm not going," he said.

Hunter glared at Tad for a moment before motioning for the others to follow him.

As he sat in silence, Tad thought this must have been similar to the meetings that were held in the 1950s and 60s, except then everyone donned a hooded white sheet before leaving. He stood and walked out of the cabin. He doubted that he would be invited again.

*****

There was a vacant lot next to the house where Terrell Smith lived with his mother. Hunter parked on the street behind the lot, far enough from Terrell's house that he wouldn't see the truck. They walked to the middle of the vacant lot which had waist-high weeds growing wildly, except for a short driveway a few feet from the boundary with the Smith property. They didn't wait long before seeing the headlights of Terrell's car approaching. Crouching in the high weeds; Hunter handed each a stocking cap with eye and nose cut-outs which they placed over their heads.

As he got out of his car, Terrell heard a noise coming from the vacant lot. He headed toward the porch, but heard the sound again. It sounded like someone moaning. He walked toward the sound.

As he entered the high weeds at the end of the drive, Hunter and Bradley Hankins attacked him from both sides. He barely had time to swing his right arm backwards toward Hunter before he was on the ground being kicked. He rolled into a ball, attempting to protect his face and groin, but the others had joined the fray.

"You need to learn to keep your mouth shut, Smith. Folks don't like you trying to turn everyone against the Hansen family." Hunter stepped back while the others continued to batter Terrell's bloodied body. "This ain't half the ass-whippin' you're going to get next time."

The men stepped away and Terrell's body relaxed slightly as he realized the onslaught had ended; but then Hunter stepped up and aimed a final kick directly at the side of his head. It landed with a sickening thud. Terrell lost consciousness and the men ran to the truck.

The next morning, Sheriff Jackson stood beside the hospital bed talking to Terrell Smith.

"Did you recognize any of them?" he asked.

"Now, how do you think I can do that? I told you they were all wearing stocking caps over their faces." Terrell didn't care for white folks generally, and the badge on the Sheriff's chest added to his irritation.

The Sheriff remained calm as he continued, "Did you hear their voices? Anything about the clothes they were wearing? Did you see a car?"

"Look, man, I know that Hunter Hansen and his buddies did it. I can't prove it and you wouldn't do anything if I could." Terrell turned his back toward his visitor.

The Sheriff left the hospital and drove downtown. He parked in front of the bank where Hobart Hansen maintained an office. As he walked toward the entrance, Tanner called his name. The Sheriff turned to see him walking across the street.

"Hello, Tanner. How have you been?" The Sheriff extended his hand and the two men shook.

"I'm doing fine. Thought I would ask if there's any news on the Terrell Smith case yet. I heard you were at the hospital earlier."

Sheriff Jackson knew that his activities were well monitored in the small town. He often joked that with a rumor mill as efficient as the one in Success, there was no need for a newspaper.

"Terrell can't identify anyone. Not much to go on other than speculation." The Sheriff liked Tanner and didn't think his interest in the case was unusual, just an old cop still chasing leads.

65

"I know you don't need my advice, but just to be blunt, Hunter Hansen is a time bomb. You better find a way to get him off the streets, and soon, Sheriff, or we'll be burying someone else who crosses his path." Tanner was blunt in his assessment.

"I'd be careful about making statements like that, Tanner, unless you've got some proof." The Sheriff turned and walked into the bank.

His visit with Hobart Hansen took little time. The secretary showed him to Hobart's office and he entered.

"Sheriff, if you're here to talk about my son, I have nothing to say. Don't take my family on as a cause. You'll get caught up in something you can't win. This community doesn't need a sheriff who helps stir up controversy and the same goes for your friend you were talking to out on the sidewalk. What's his name, Tanner?"

"Hobart, I won't ask you about your son, but I'll tell you this. There's more people in this town than just me that believe if you don't get a handle on his behavior, there are some bad days ahead for him and you. I'm not talking to you as a sheriff, but as a father." The Sheriff turned and left the bank.

As Hansen sat in his office watching the Sheriff walk away, he realized that the warning was worth considering. Hunter had always been wild, but recent events made his father worry that things might be spinning out of control.

No charges were filed in the assault on Terrell Smith. He spent a week in the hospital and left in time to lead the rally in front of the Hansen bank. The rally consisted of ten people. The beating had struck fear in the hearts of some. For others, they just didn't want to anger people like Hobart Hansen. He and his friends signed a lot of weekly paychecks in Fulshear County.

Chapter 10

Life in Success returned to normal for most of its residents. The murder wasn't forgotten and when people got together to visit, the discussion sometimes turned to 'that girl's murder,' but few spent much time dwelling on what had happened. Estelle Parker, Calvin Thibodaux and Terrell Smith were three exceptions. As a result, Milo Tanner couldn't let it go either.

Estelle grieved privately. She never talked about her daughter to anyone. After two sessions with a psychologist in Houston, she told Thibodaux she was through.

"I appreciate what you're trying to do, Calvin, but nothing's going to bring my baby back. I just got to live with it."

Thibodaux worried about her, but he left her to grieve as she chose. He checked in twice each week and continued to take care of her lawn and other chores. He never discussed the murder with her. Thibodaux had not forgotten it though. He intended to make it right; at least he had to try.

When Terrell Smith recovered from the beating, he had new energy for the campaign, *Justice for Danielle*. He continued to organize rallies, although they were sparsely attended. Terrell tried several times to get Estelle and Thibodaux to join him at the rallies, but neither of them would make public appearances with him.

Three months after Terrell was released from the hospital, Thibodaux and Tanner were sitting in Tanner's backyard admiring Thibodaux's yard work.

"I was just curious, Tanner. Did you ever think of some other way we can make this deal right with Hunter Hansen? You know I haven't let it go."

Tanner wasn't surprised, but he was out of answers. "Thibodaux, sometimes you just have to wait. I don't think he's ever going to pay for Danielle's murder. But a guy like him keeps screwing up his whole life. Sooner or later he'll get his."

"Well, Tanner, I hear what you're saying, but there are some folks around here still waiting on his daddy to get his. I'm not sure you got this one right. It may be time for somebody to make their own justice."

"Thibodaux, why are you talking like that? You'd never get away with it. You wouldn't enjoy the rest of your life in prison or worse."

Tanner reached out and placed his hand on Thibodaux's shoulder.

Shrugging it off, Thibodaux said, "I won't let this go. If there's no way to get the law to do something, I will."

"Okay, Thibodaux, but before you do anything like that, let me go visit with the D.A. one more time and see what he says."

Tanner knew the answer, but he wanted Thibodaux to slow down. The next day Tanner went to the District Attorney's office. He had to wait 30 minutes before Jack Sadosky stepped into the waiting area and invited him into his office.

"Mr. Tanner, what can I do for you?" Sadosky began.

"I came by to talk to you about the Danielle Parker murder case. I thought you might tell me what the status is."

"What exactly is your interest, Mr. Tanner? You obviously are not a member of the family." Sadosky sat back in his chair.

The D.A.'s tone did not set well with Tanner. "Let's just say I'm a citizen who's interested in seeing justice done. Does that clear up *who I am?*"

Sadosky held both hands palm out in front of his chest. "Hold on, Tanner. I'm not your enemy here. I just thought it would be helpful to know exactly what your interest is."

"I'm a concerned citizen who happens to be a friend of Danielle's uncle. That family is grieving over her death and the fact that Hunter Hansen isn't being prosecuted. Aside from Danielle's case, he seems to bring trouble with him everywhere he goes. Is there any possibility that he might be charged with her murder, the beating of Terrell Smith, or anything else in this county?"

Although Tanner understood the legal intricacies that made it unlikely that this D.A. or any other could convict Hunter of Danielle's murder, his frustration and concern for his friend caused his aggressiveness.

"Mr. Tanner, I've been told you are a retired detective, is that right?"

"I'm retired from Houston," Tanner responded.

"Then you know that we don't take cases to court unless we have enough evidence to warrant a trial. Hell, in this case there wasn't even enough evidence to indict Hunter. Regarding your personal opinions of him, I'd suggest you be very careful when you make accusations. Someone may call your hand and demand proof. Now unless there's something else I can help you with, I need to get to work." Sadosky stood.

Tanner left the office. He was not surprised by what he'd been told, but it didn't help his dilemma of how to advise Thibodaux.

Two hours later Tanner walked into First State Bank, where he conducted his local banking business. It was the Hansen family-owned bank.

As he was making a deposit with one of the tellers, Hobart Hansen walked up and stood beside him.

"Mr. Tanner. We are happy that you selected our bank to do business here locally. I haven't met you, but I've been hearing quite a lot about you. Do you have a moment to step into my office?"

Too curious to say no, Tanner nodded and said, "Sure, just let me finish my business here."

Hansen stood to the side until the teller handed the receipt to Tanner after which he followed the banker into his office.

"Have a seat, Mr. Tanner. Can I have my secretary get you a cold drink or coffee?"

"No thanks. I'll be fine," Tanner said as he sat in one of the two chairs in front of Hansen's desk.

"I understand you've been making some inquiries with the Sheriff and the District Attorney regarding my son. I wanted to talk to you to see if there's anything I can help you with."

Hansen was smooth, Tanner thought. He must be boiling inside, but it didn't show.

"I'm not sure what you mean, Mr. Hansen. I met with both the D.A. and the Sheriff to get an update on the death of Danielle Parker. We discussed your son, because there's quite a circumstantial case indicating that he's the murderer." Tanner saw Hansen's ears turn red. "So, as I said, I'm not quite sure what you're asking."

It must have been difficult, Tanner thought, but Hansen remained cool.

"Mr. Tanner. My son is no murderer. You are aware, I'm sure, that he was not indicted by the grand jury and that a number of his friends have told the police where he was the night that tragic incident occurred.

"Now, although I know both Ms. Parker and Mr. Thibodaux, it is only an acquaintance. If either

73

of them is suffering financially during this time of grief, I will be happy to assist them.

"As I understand the investigation, it is over. I hope that the murderer is caught and prosecuted, but I really don't want to hear any further accusations against my son."

Tanner stood and placed both his hands on the other man's desk.

"Ms. Parker and Mr. Thibodaux want justice for their daughter and niece, not money. As for your son, and how well you know Estelle, what about the daughter you never recognized as yours? Whether you think Hunter murdered your daughter, Danielle Parker, or not, he needs your help, not your money and influence. If you don't help him get a handle on his life, you'll come to regret it and you will have lost two children instead of just one. Good day, Mr. Hansen."

Tanner walked back to the teller with whom he had made the deposit earlier and closed his account before leaving.

*****

Hobart Hansen felt tension in his jaw, chest and hands. He breathed deeply through his mouth, consciously trying to relax. He stretched and wiggled his fingers, noticing the circulation returning, then pressed the intercom button on his phone, "Patty, bring me a cup of coffee, please."

Within minutes, a petite young brunette with smooth tan skin Hobart liked to admire, had placed a blue mug, sporting the bank's logo, filled with steaming black coffee in front of him. "Will that be all, Mr. Hansen?" She acknowledged Hobart's brief glance and head shake with a timid smile, turned and left the room.

Hobart glanced up, gazing at her back as she walked away. It was a game he played. The young woman worked at being professional – even in her walk. He'd noticed though, that when distracted, there was a natural sway of her hips in her stride.

Swaying hips had always attracted him. One could have put music to Estelle's sway when she was a teen. He had noticed that the summer he came home from college without his wife and son.

Hobart had stopped by to check on his grandmother, bedridden with cancer. Rosa, Estelle's mother, had been called to help care for her and had left her own prescriptions at home. When Estelle arrived with Rosa's medicines, Hobart welcomed his childhood playmate with delight.

Being separated while he was away at college didn't seem to affect the long friendship. They had known each other all their lives. Rosa had worked at Hobart's grandparents' country home as a house maid. At times when Rosa had no one to leave Estelle with, she was allowed to accompany her mother to her job.

As young children they had colored pages or put puzzles together at Rosa's feet as she ironed. There had been special times when his family rested after lunch that Rosa entertained young Hobart and Estelle by telling them stories under the shade of a large oak in the back yard. She taught them how to take turns, pushing one another in the swing dangling from a limb of the old tree. She even taught the children how to catch perch in the pond near their house!

Once when they were sitting on the bank watching the red and white plastic corks bobbing in the water, Hobart noticed the sun glinting on her face. "Oh 'Stell', your skin is catchin' a sunbeam! I see gold in it!"

Hobart's sixth birthday party was to be a big event! There would be pony and cart rides, games, balloons, cake and ice cream! Hobart excitedly explained to his playmate that it would be fun for her too.

Rosa's eyes left her task and met those of his grandmother. That evening Grandmother had explained, "Children from the quarters have their own parties. They don't go to parties that white children have." It was confusing to Hobart.

Estelle stopped coming to play at Grandmother's. Hobart was lonely at first. But a whole new world of friends opened up when he started school that year.

The renewal of their friendship upon Hobart's return from college had begun innocently enough with walks around the land where they played and learned how to fish. Once, he insisted on swinging her under the old shade tree. Careless touches during swinging ignited familiar sensations for Hobart. He'd become used to a physical bond and missed "the thrill of it all".

During their 'catching-up' conversations, Estelle mentioned casual dating relationships, but no steady boyfriends. Rosa had always encouraged her to get an education that would enable her to work somewhere other than as someone's housemaid. Estelle knew he had married Vanessa Brown, but he told her that was over and she wanted to believe him.

The happiness and trust developed during their childhood years renewed a relationship that led to a summer romance. Hobart began meeting his old friend, who still lived in the "quarters", discreetly. By summer's end, they had become consumed with one another.

He and Estelle were drawn to one another, but he knew she would never fit into his world. Caring for her became risky once she became pregnant. He already had more responsibility to deal with than he cared for. Upon his father's urging, he'd offered her money to end it; that was the last time he ever met with her. She'd betrayed him by throwing the money in his face. To Hobart, the child became her problem at that moment. He packed his bags and returned to his wife and child with no remorse.

****

Danielle's paternity had become a problem that others seem to know about now! Tanner's reference to her bothered him more than he wanted it to. Until now, he'd never really thought of the girl as "his child" much less, acknowledged her as such.

His head began to ache as his thoughts came quickly. *I am a good father to Hunter. He has everything I could give him, and a better future than most. But he stays in trouble!! Somehow I have to help him grow up. Marriage seemed to help me settle down more. Maybe that's what he needs.*

*****

A month later, Vanessa and Hobart Hansen joined Mr. and Mrs. Rand Boatwright in announcing the marriage of Hunter Hansen to the Boatwrights' daughter, Camilla. It would be an enormous wedding, after which the bride and groom would spend a month in Europe. Upon returning home to Success, Hunter Hansen would begin work at First State Bank as a loan officer.

Hunter and Camilla had known each other since childhood and dated a few times when arranged by one parent or the other, usually to accompany one another to a social event. Not unattractive, but rather plain, Camilla had never had a serious suitor. This was in no small part due to her extremely introverted personality. Hunter had never given any consideration to her even as a friend.

During Hobart Hansen's very frank discussion with Hunter, prompted by his conversations with the Sheriff and Tanner, he suggested Camilla might be the right person for his son to consider settling down with. Hobart knew that Rand Boatwright worried that his daughter would become an old maid and told Hunter that.

Hunter accepted his father's advice because he sensed that he was close to losing the financial support he relied on from his father. He called Camilla for what he described as taking her on a real date; she accepted. Two weeks later their wedding was announced.

*****

The wedding became the social event of the season for the small town. Gossip concerning Danielle's death was muted by the celebrations and planning regarding the marriage. The very atmosphere in Success seemed filled with romance and well-wishers. Hobart was relieved, appreciating the unexpected positive effects of the announcement. *Perhaps people really do love a wedding,* he thought.

The honeymoon was his gift. Soon the newlyweds were touring Europe, but the seams began coming apart on the marriage during the first two weeks. One reason that Hunter had never been successful in long-term relationships was his proclivity for unusual sexual activity. He was a sadist. Camilla learned about his sexual tendencies only ten days into her marriage to Hunter. By the time they returned to Success from the honeymoon, her body was covered with dark bruises. Camilla faced some difficult decisions as she began trying to live the role of the newlywed.

It was stressful and embarrassing; she was close to an emotional collapse. Nevertheless, two weeks after returning from her honeymoon, Camilla had moved back home with her parents, the divorce had been filed and Hunter Hansen was attempting to convince his father that it was not his fault. He was also going to work at the bank every day and showing an interest in learning to be a loan officer. Hunter knew that his free ride was coming to an end, especially if he failed to impress Hobart Hansen of his sincerity this time.

Soon everyone in Success had a story. Nearly all the rumors involved violence on Hunter's part. Once the divorce was filed, Tanner went to the courthouse and pulled the divorce petition. He was not surprised to see that the cause was simply 'irreconcilable differences.' There was no mention of physical violence.

Chapter 11

The day after the Hansen and Boatwright families had announced the wedding of Hunter and Camilla, Tanner told Thibodaux the details of his visit with the District Attorney and the conversation with Hobart Hansen. They sat in Tanner's backyard and sipped a beer as he talked. When he had finished, he paused but a moment.

"Thibodaux, I want you to give me your word that you won't do anything about this for the time being. Give me a few days. I promise you that if I can't come up with a better plan, I'll help you do it your way."

Tanner knew he was making a commitment that went against everything he had stood for since becoming a police officer. But he was sure he could find a way to convince the District Attorney to prosecute Hunter Hansen or that Hunter would screw something else up bad enough that the D.A. would have to prosecute. He had to find an alternative to Thibodaux's revenge!

"Tanner, I told you before that you are an unusual man. You don't have to do anything else for me. I'll give you some time, mainly because I'd rather do about anything than to kill another man, but you have to understand- it's not over."

*****

For Tanner, the days flew by more quickly than any other such period of his life. He had called on both the Sheriff and the District Attorney. Both had made it clear that Danielle's murder would likely go unsolved. But he wasn't without a plan when he and Thibodaux had another of their backyard meetings.

"I want to talk to you about a plan, Thibodaux. I know you have been patient by giving me time to think about this. Hunter Hansen is not going to be prosecuted for Danielle's murder. But I'll help you put him away.

"Guys like Hunter don't change. He'll hurt someone else. We need to watch him so that next time he doesn't beat the system, even if it means we become witnesses to whatever he does. I'm retired and your work allows you a lot of latitude in setting your hours. Let's try to stay on him from the time he leaves his apartment until we put him to bed at night.

"Now, with just the two of us, we won't be able to tail him 24-7, but we'll try for a couple of weeks until his wedding so we understand his routine. Then, when he gets back from his honeymoon, we'll just watch him at times we think he's most likely to step over the line. How's that sound to you?"

Thibodaux didn't hesitate, "You know, Tanner, I'm sure you mean well, but do you really think a Hansen is ever going to be held accountable in this county? I'm all for following him, catching him screwing up, and helping to prosecute him, but I just don't see it working."

Tanner ignored the question and the comment.

"Then let's work out a schedule for the next couple of weeks. This may take a while, but we'll make it work."

For the next two weeks, they followed Hunter just as they had Jeremy Crocker. Hunter's daytime routine was predictable. He left his apartment a few minutes before nine each weekday morning and arrived at the bank a few minutes after the bank opened.

He sat at a desk, dealing with customers who were applying for loans until about eleven each morning, at which time he would leave for lunch. He usually ate at Tex's BBQ, sometimes with friends, occasionally with his father. If he wasn't with his father, the lunch would often stretch to two hours or even longer. The afternoons at the bank were the same, with Hunter always leaving by four.

Although Hunter's wedding was fast approaching, his nights and weekends didn't reflect a deep commitment to his betrothed. During the two weeks of surveillance, he visited his fiancé's home twice, and stayed only a couple of hours each time.

Most week nights he was at the *Dry Gulch Saloon* until closing, sometimes stumbling through the parking lot, so drunk he could barely drive home.

On several occasions when Tanner or Thibodaux followed him home, Hunter passed out before getting out of his truck. When that happened, he was usually still there when the sun peeked over the top of the apartment building.

On both Saturday nights, he picked up local hangers on from the bar and took each to his apartment. The women left after a couple of hours and neither spent the night. The two friends concluded that Sundays were presumably Hunter's detox days, as they rarely saw him leave his apartment at all on the Sabbath.

*****

The initial surveillance had ended just when preparations began for the wedding. Tanner and Thibodaux relaxed until the newly-wed Hansen couple returned from their much talked about honeymoon.

Thibodaux was still not optimistic. "Do you really think when Hunter returns a married man, that we'll ever catch him screwing up enough to make him pay?" he asked.

"I'm not sure, my friend, but I know people like him don't change because of wedding vows. I'm committed to continue trying."

Of course neither man knew then that within two weeks of returning to Success from his honeymoon, Hunter Hansen would once again be single.

*****

Once the newly married couple returned and Camilla unexpectedly ended the marriage, Tanner and Thibodaux began again to monitor Hunter's nighttime activity. They watched his apartment as friends and acquaintances came and went. One night a young lady who visited regularly entered the apartment and within an hour she left hurriedly.

Thibodaux happened to be watching the apartment that night and could clearly see that she was sobbing and holding her left arm with her right. After some difficulty, she managed to get into her car and drive away. Thibodaux followed her as she drove to the small community hospital.

The next morning, as Tanner and Thibodaux drank coffee in Tanner's back yard, Thibodaux mentioned the incident he'd witnessed. Though neither man knew her name, Thibodaux recognized her as a frequent customer at the *Dry Gulch Saloon*. Tanner decided to have a beer or two that afternoon to see what he might learn. At three o'clock he was sitting on a stool talking with the barmaid. He was the only customer there.

"Your name's Tanner, right?" Sheila asked as she placed the beer in front of him.

"That's right and you're Sheila. I guess I'm becoming a regular if you remember my name."

"You've been in often enough for me to remember. Of course, in a town as small as Success, it's not a big challenge to remember everyone who walks in, even if it's just once." Sheila wiped the bar as she talked.

"Yeah, I guess it can get pretty boring around here. Not much excitement. But then that's why people move to small towns." Tanner scratched at the label on his beer.

"That's usually the case, but we've had a little excitement the last couple of days. Do you know Chrystal Jansen who hangs out here most weekends?"

Sheila's comment got Tanner's attention, but he merely shrugged his shoulders as if he wasn't sure.

"You'd know her if you saw her. She's been here when you come in. Anyway, she's in a world of shit now. She made the mistake of going home with Hunter the other night. You know Hunter Hansen, I'm sure. Everybody does.

"She ended up in the emergency room with a broken arm and her shoulder out of its socket. She should have known better. Hunter's a mean son-of-a-bitch when he's drinking." Sheila chuckled, "Hell, some of his former girl friends say he doesn't have to be drinking. He's just mean all the time."

Tanner tried not to show much interest in the conversation, but said, "Well, I hope she's okay. A shoulder injury can really be painful."

"Oh, it's not the shoulder that's the problem. The Sheriff showed up at the hospital and she told him what happened. She agreed to file charges on Hunter. Chrystal isn't from around here. She didn't understand that in Fulshear County, you don't take on the Hansen family. You can't win that fight."

"Really? What do you think will happen?" Tanner asked.

"Well, if she's lucky, Hunter's dad will pay her to drop the charges and move away. If she's not so lucky, Hunter may break her other arm, but either way, she won't be around here much longer."

"Doesn't sound like a pleasant experience," Tanner said, finishing his beer. "I guess she'll figure it out. Thanks for the conversation and the beer."

Chapter 12

The next morning Tanner went to the post office to send a package to a friend in Houston. As he was leaving, he met the Sheriff making his daily run to pick up mail.

"Morning, Sheriff," Tanner said.

"Tanner. I'm surprised you haven't been to my office. I figured you must have heard the latest on Hunter Hansen."

The Sheriff leaned against the hand-rail at the top of the steps.

"Yeah, what's that all about, Sheriff?" Tanner didn't acknowledge having heard about the charges.

"Well, not much really. A young woman ended up at the hospital a couple of nights ago. She said Hunter attacked her when she went with him to his apartment. She gave the investigator some pretty lurid details of some of his sexual demands.

"The rest is pretty standard. She filed charges and then came back this morning wanting to withdraw her complaint. Said she's moving to Dallas. You can draw your own conclusions."

The Sheriff looked down at the sidewalk as he finished speaking.

"So normally this is where I would say, *Sheriff, what's it going to take to get Hunter Hansen put away, a murder?*, but then that's already happened. What about the D.A. convening a grand jury to investigate a criminal conspiracy? Call in all the witnesses and families who have been paid to leave town. Put some pressure in the right place and somebody will break. You think it could happen?"

Tanner already knew the answer, but he wanted the Sheriff to say it.

"This D.A. isn't going to do that. He won't pick a fight with Hobart Hansen unless he's sure of the outcome. It's a shame, but it's also a fact."

The Sheriff pushed off the hand-rail and headed for the post office entry. "Welcome to small town Texas, Tanner."

Tanner knew that his life had just changed. Thibodaux was right. If there would be justice for Danielle, it would be at the hands of Thibodaux and Tanner.

*****

Tanner went from the post office to Tex's World Famous BBQ, where he scarfed down a large lunch of pork ribs, potato salad and cold slaw. He drank two beers with his meal and read the local newspaper. It was a weekly, so most of the news was already known by those who were interested, but it kept Tanner busy as he finished the second beer.

When he finished, he drove the three blocks to the *Dry Gulch Saloon*. It was a sunny, fall afternoon, a perfect day to drink beer in the shade of a large oak tree that grew on the side of the building. Two elderly life-long residents of Success had the same idea and were sitting at the picnic table that was placed under the shade tree for just that purpose. Tanner had met them both on previous trips to the saloon, so he walked inside, ordered three beers, and approached them.

"You fellows mind if I join you," he said, placing a beer in front of each man.

"Not if you come bearing gifts," Jack Calahan responded, reaching for the beer.

Tanner sat at the table next to Calahan's drinking partner, Rudy Blazik.

"So have you two solved any major world problems yet today?" Tanner asked with a smile.

"No sir. We were waiting on someone to come along, buy us a beer, and suggest just such a problem we might consider," Calahan responded. "My Pollock buddy here, Rudy, is just the guy for such a task."

All three men laughed. Rudy held his beer out and the three touched bottles in a toast.

"So, Tanner, have you settled into rural life yet? Are you missing the big city?" Calahan continued.

"I'm enjoying the quiet life. No question this was a good move for me," Tanner replied.

"Well, there's been more excitement since you moved here than in the last ten years, what with a murder, that black kid getting beat up, and now I understand the Hansen kid is in another pickle over how he treated that pretty little thing, Chrystal. You know her, don't you? She hangs out here on week-ends. You hear about that, Tanner?"

"Sheila told me yesterday. I guess Chrystal will just have to pick her boyfriends a little better." Tanner tried to appear uninterested.

"Yeah, that boy's pretty wild. Most of us old timers thought his dad, Hobart, was wild, but he was an amateur compared to Hunter. Hell, Hobart chased the girls, both sides of the tracks, but there was a line he never crossed. Never got rough with the girls, at least that anyone knows, and never drank himself silly like that boy of his does. Hell, I've woke him up a half dozen times passed out in his pick-up truck when I drive by here in the mornings." Calahan loved to gossip.

Rudy, who was much less loquacious than Calahan, weighed in, "My nephew lives in those apartments that Hansen owns. Hunter stays there too; I guess Hobart gives him a free apartment to keep from having to put up with him living at home. Anyway, my nephew tells me that once every couple of weeks, one of the tellers from the bank has to come over and wake Hunter up to go to work. Funny thing is, he's usually passed out in his pick-up truck and they have a hell of a time getting him awake. Everybody that lives there comes out to watch the show."

Tanner continued the conversation with the two old men for over two hours. Each of them bought a round of beers and Tanner bought a second round. They discussed national politics; both Rudy and Calahan hated Obama. They talked about the weather, and finally, inevitably, they discussed the prospects for the Success High School football team, the Tigers. Tanner finished the fourth beer; his limit when he had to drive. He left the two engaged in a conversation about the merits of the current county judge.

*****

Tanner parked his car in the driveway and went into the house. He was putting off the conversation he knew he must have with Thibodaux. The two men were close friends. Thibodaux had told him about some of the experiences of being an Army Ranger, especially the time he'd spent in the Middle East. Tanner knew that Thibodaux was a man who could be counted on, no matter what the mission.

But Tanner knew that once he, himself, crossed the threshold and took justice into his own hands, his life would change forever. Hundreds of times when he was a cop and saw murderers and child molesters escape the punishment of the courts, he had considered how satisfying it would be to right the wrong himself.

And many times, when he worked a case and filed charges on a suspect, he would think how careless the crook had been, a cigarette dropped at the scene, a witness who had not been anticipated, or an ego that mandated he brag about his crime. If Tanner was a crook, he knew he wouldn't make the amateur mistakes. Like many investigators, he believed he could commit the perfect crime.

However, he had never really considered that he would actually engage in a crime or mete out justice himself. That changed when he made the commitment to his friend that Danielle would get justice.

Tanner went to bed early that night, after calling Thibodaux and asking him to take a ride with him the following morning. At seven Tanner pulled into Thibodaux's drive and honked the horn. Holding two cups of coffee, Thibodaux walked to the car and handed one cup to Tanner, before getting in.

The two men sipped their coffee in silence as Tanner drove out of town. He veered off Farm Road 109 as they approached the Colorado River and drove to the spot where Danielle's body had been found. He parked under the bridge and the two men continued to sip their coffee, each lost in his own thoughts for a few minutes.

Finally Thibodaux spoke. "They're not going to get Hunter Hansen on this latest deal with the girl, are they, Tanner?"

"Nope, she's leaving town just like the others. You were right. It's time to fix this thing with Hunter ourselves. I know what to do and how to do it. You must understand, though, that it's something we can't take back. I just want to be sure you understand."

"Tanner, I loved that little girl. I'm not a crusader. I don't stand up and shout to the world how things aren't fair. The Hansen family hurt Estelle while I was away making a career in the army. Twenty years later, I came back and saw the same thing, except this time it's worse. Whatever happens, Hunter's going to pay for what he did to Danielle. But why are you taking on my fight?"

"I'm really not," Tanner began. "I spent a lifetime thinking I was doing a good thing by being a cop. I always played by the rules. Then one day I got a case on my desk that turned my life upside down.

"A little seven-year-old girl was raped and murdered. I worked the case until the point that a District Court Judge's twenty-five year old son became the only suspect. When I took the case to the D.A. to get a warrant for the Judge's son, the D.A. stalled and told me to come back the next day. The next morning, the case was reassigned to another detective.

"I knew why they pulled me off the case, but I didn't say anything. The detective who got the case let it lay. Three weeks later, a patrol car got a call about someone being in an abandoned building one night. When they got there, they found the judge's son kneeling over another little girl. He had hacked her body to pieces.

"He never went to trial; instead he went straight to a mental hospital. I retired knowing if I had raised hell about being pulled off the case, I might have saved that second little girl. I'm doing this for my own redemption."

Tanner looked as if he had run a marathon by the time he stopped talking. His face was drawn and his breathing came in short, tortured gulps. Both men got out of the car and walked along the river bank, neither saying anything. They sat on a fallen tree trunk next to the river and Tanner told Thibodaux about his plan to kill Hunter Hansen.

Chapter 13

Things weren't going so well for Hunter Hansen. After Hobart paid Chrystal Jansen $50,000 to move away and drop charges against his son, he laid down the law to Hunter as he had never spoken to him before.

This would be the last bailout. No longer was Hunter a loan officer at the bank. He returned to being a trainee bank teller. Hobart made it clear that he was to be at work on time and stay until his supervisor released him.

"The consequences for not complying with these instructions are very simple," Hobart told him. "One slip-up and you lose your job, your apartment, and your relationship with this family. Don't fuck it up, Hunter! This time it's for real."

Hunter knew he had hit the limit. Never doubting the sweet deal he had; he intended to protect it. During the work week he was a new man. Arriving at work on the early teller shift fifteen minutes before the drive-thru opened at eight, he made a real effort to be an effective employee.

Weekends, however, were another matter. While Hunter stayed home or visited his parents for dinner on week nights, he was at the *Dry Gulch Saloon* or a bar in one of the neighboring communities every Friday and Saturday night. He shot pool with his buddies, drank heavily, and, though not as often as before, still passed out in his truck occasionally, either in the parking lot at the bar or his apartment.

He did make one concession. Though he didn't recognize his treatment of women as a problem, he knew that another complaint to the authorities would be the end of the relationship with his father. So he stopped dating and picking up women at the bars. He saw this as a temporary inconvenience, and became angry when he thought about how the women in his life caused all his problems.

*****

Tanner and Thibodaux quickly figured out Hunter's routine. It was much simpler for them than they had anticipated. On Friday and Saturday nights at a little before midnight they met at Tanner's home, then drove together to the *Dry Gulch Saloon.* They parked a half block from the bar and waited for it to close. When Hunter Hansen came out they followed him home. They stayed until he went into his apartment, after which they ended their night of surveillance.

This game of cat and mouse continued for six weeks. Tanner began to believe that Hunter must have cut back on his drinking. When they watched him walk to his car, he seemed to have little trouble.

"Do you think we need a new plan," Thibodaux asked, on the sixth Saturday night they had followed him home.

"No," replied Tanner, "he has a behavior pattern that has been a predictable routine for a long time. This last encounter with Chrystal and his dad's intervention on his behalf was probably a wake-up call. There's no telling what kind of threats his dad has hanging over his head after that, but he'll fall back into his routine if we're patient."

As if Tanner was psychic, the next Friday night Hunter staggered out of the *Dry Gulch Saloon* at exactly midnight. He leaned against the fender of a car for a moment to get his bearings. Swaying from side to side, Hunter made it to his pick-up truck. He stood beside the door trying to insert the key into the lock for over a minute. Finally, he opened the door and crawled into the truck.

The two observers watched as Hunter sat behind the wheel and tried to insert the key into the ignition switch. In a few moments, his movements stopped and he slumped over the steering wheel. Tanner and Thibodaux waited until the other patrons left and the bartender locked up.

As the bartender was walking to her car, she saw Hunter passed out. She opened the door and attempted to wake him, but soon gave up and drove away.

"Well, at least we know that he's back to his old habit of drinking more than he can handle," Thibodaux commented. "It shouldn't be long now."

"We just need for him to keep control a little longer," Tanner replied. "He needs to pass out once he pulls into his apartment parking lot."

On the following two Saturday nights, Hunter passed out in his truck at the bar's parking lot. Finally, on the third Saturday, he stumbled to his truck, managed to open the door, start the engine and drive away. Swerving from one side of the road to the other, Tanner and Thibodaux were worried that he might end up in a ditch before arriving at his apartment, but he somehow managed.

He pulled into the same parking spot that he often used, cut the engine and opened the driver's door. But then his movements slowed and soon he was once again slumped over the steering wheel, passed out.

It was time for action. Tanner drove the car a block from the parking lot. Both men donned surgical gloves and hooded sweaters. Thibodaux grabbed a large duffel bag from the floor in front of him as they quietly exited the car and approached the rear of Hunter's truck. From the bag, Thibodaux pulled a long vacuum sweeper hose with a metal sleeve taped to one end. He placed the metal sleeve over the exhaust pipe of Hunter's truck and reached into the bag once more, retrieving a roll of duct tape.

He quickly taped the metal sleeve to the hot exhaust pipe.

Tanner stretched the other end of the vacuum hose to the driver's door. He rolled the window down slightly and placed the hose end inside the truck. He then reached across the steering wheel, underneath Hunter's slumped torso and started the engine. Hunter stirred slightly when the engine started, grunted and coughed, then relaxed, once again slumped against the steering wheel.

Tanner slowly shut the driver's door and the two men gathered the bag, made sure nothing but the roll of duct tape was left at the scene and walked back to Tanner's car. Five minutes later they arrived at Tanner's home.

"Okay, partner. If nothing goes wrong, Mr. Hunter Hansen's obituary should be in the paper soon. Anything we missed?" Tanner asked.

"No. Just like you said, the vacuum cleaner hose came from the city dump. You bought the duct tape in Austin. We brought everything back with us except the roll of duct tape because a suicide victim doesn't get a chance to clean up after himself," Thibodaux said.

"That's right and there were no witnesses at the scene that we know of. If anyone saw us, all they could make out was two guys with hoodies over their heads. You're welcome to grab a nap on the couch if you'd rather not drive home," Tanner replied, nodding toward the couch.

"I appreciate it, but I'm going home and have a short conversation with Danielle. I'm going to tell her I didn't forget." Thibodaux stood and took a step closer to Tanner embracing him in a bear hug. "Thank you, my friend. I can never repay you."

With that he was gone.

*****

The following morning there was a flurry of police activity in the Hansen-owned apartment project. City police strung yellow crime-scene tape around the entire parking lot. Photos were taken and the body was removed. Sheriff Jackson appeared on the scene, sort of a courtesy call in case the city police needed help. Hobart Hansen arrived minutes later.

"No suicide note in the truck?" the Sheriff asked one of the uniformed officers.

"No sir," the officer responded.

The Sheriff turned to Hobart Hansen. "Mr. Hansen, do you have a key to Hunter's apartment?"

Hansen was having trouble coming to grips with the idea of his son's death. He stared absently at the Sheriff. Finally, he seemed to regain his senses.

"Yes, I have a master key for all the locks. Here, it's on my key chain." He handed the keys to the Sheriff.

The Sheriff and the police officer entered the apartment, and discovered an even bigger surprise than Hunter's death. Stuffed in the closet of his bedroom was the body of Chrystal Jansen. She had been strangled after what appeared to be a brutal beating.

The investigation was completed, although some of the details were left to speculation simply because the only suspect in the murder of Chrystal was also dead. The report stated that she had been dead about thirty six hours before discovery and that she had been killed in the apartment, more specifically in Hunter's bedroom.

It was presumed that Hunter had enticed her to his apartment late on Friday afternoon, probably with the promise of even more money before she left town. She was then murdered before he left for his usual Friday night drinking binge at the *Dry Gulch Saloon*. After a second night of drinking on Saturday night, with the body still stuffed in his closet, he had a twinge of conscience and committed suicide by carbon monoxide poisoning.

Although there was much speculation and gossip about conspiracy theories, neither Tanner nor Thibodaux was ever mentioned as being involved. The two persons most often linked with the conspiracy advocates were Hobart Hansen, who some speculated had reached his wits end with Hunter's antics, and Terrell Smith, the young crusader against the injustice of Hunter Hansen never being held accountable for Danielle's death. But in the end, the District Attorney accepted the murder/suicide story as the most likely course of events, tied neatly in a package with two cleared cases on the record.

Chapter 14

Six months later, Sheriff Jackson and Tanner sat in Jackson's office drinking coffee.

"Tanner, what'd you think about the Hansen suicide case? Did anything strike you as unusual about it?" The Sheriff leaned back in his chair.

"Well, Randy, I guess I don't know enough about it to answer that. Everything I heard, except for a few of the folks who think there was a conspiracy, is that Hunter murdered the girl and then killed himself. No reason for me to question that."

"Did anyone ever let you see the crime scene photos? I thought maybe you would have been interested since you went after Hunter pretty hard on Danielle's murder." The Sheriff reached in a drawer of his desk.

"I never asked anyone about the case, Randy. I'll admit I think his death is a fitting end to Danielle's murder, but it's not my business."

Tanner took a sip of coffee as the Sheriff laid a large manila envelope on the desk in front of him.

"Take a look, anyway, just a courtesy to me. Of course, it's not my case. The City guys handled it, but I just wondered if you might see anything you thought was unusual."

The Sheriff pushed the envelope toward Tanner.

Tanner opened the envelope and spread the photos across the desk. When he saw the third photo, he knew what the Sheriff was talking about, but he concealed his knowledge well.

"I guess you'll have to help me, Randy. Maybe I'm losing my investigator's touch, but I don't see anything but a dead body and an apparatus taped up to the truck to asphyxiate its occupant."

"Would it help if I told you Hunter's alcohol level was 0.23?"

"I'm missing your point. Lot of people kill themselves when they're depressed from drinking. I don't get it." Tanner leaned back in his chair and sipped his coffee again.

The Sheriff reached for the photo of the truck's tail pipe and offered it to Tanner.

"That's a really neat job of taping up that vacuum hose for a guy that was nearly three times over the legal limit of alcohol, don't you think? Wrapped straight and cut straight. No ragged ends."

Tanner didn't respond. He had been sure he covered all the angles and here he was sitting looking at crime scene photos proving that he had not committed the perfect crime.

The Sheriff reached for the photo and said, "Not a big deal, I just thought it might interest you. Like I said it's not my case and the local cops aren't likely to question such a minor detail. The D.A. is happy to have it wrapped up. Most people in town probably thought it was poetic justice, especially after the girl's body was found in his apartment.

"I had this passing thought that maybe we had somebody out here exacting a little vigilante justice, but that's a little far-fetched in Fulshear County. Not to say there might not be a place for it from time to time."

Tanner stood, thanked the Sheriff for the coffee and left his office. The Sheriff might be suspicious, but he wasn't interested in reopening a case that had been handled by the City Police. Tanner was comfortable that the case was closed for good.

As he drove home, he thought to himself that he didn't feel bad at all about this new direction for his life. He and his new partner, Thibodaux, had righted a wrong and kept more people from suffering at the hands of Hunter Hansen. The partnership was going to be good, even if Thibodaux was a black man with a Cajun name.

COMING SOON

The second in the Tanner & Thibodaux Action Adventure Series, *RICH MAN, DEAD MAN,* is scheduled for publication soon. Look for it on my website, at Amazon, or wherever good books are sold or send an e-mail to Larry@LarryWatts.net requesting e-mail notification when it is available.

ABOUT THE AUTHOR

Larry Watts worked as a police officer for 21 years. He left that career to represent officers across Texas in employment matters, including officer involved shootings and other tragic events. He now writes novels and enjoys life on the Gulf Coast with his wife, Carolyn.

A message from Larry:

If you enjoyed this story, please let me know. I can be contacted at Larry@LarryWatts.net. You can also visit my website at www.LarryWatts.net, and connect with me on Facebook and Twitter.

Other books by Larry Watts

Right, Wrong, & Rationalizing Truth (2011)

Beautiful Revenge (a short story 2012)

Cheating Justice (2013)

The Park Place Rangers, A book of short stories (2014)

14666276R00067

Made in the USA
San Bernardino, CA
01 September 2014